NERVOUS, BABYMOUSE?

BABYMOUSE
QUEEN OF THE WORLD!

BY JENNIFER L. HOLM & MATTHEW HOLM

RANDOM HOUSE NEW YORK

WHAT IS ALL THIS STUFF?

 Published in the United States by Random House Children's Books, a division of Random House, Inc., New York, and simultaneously in Canada by Random House of Canada Limited, Toronto.

www.randomhouse.com/kids
www.babymouse.com

Library of Congress Cataloging-in-Publication Data

Holm, Jennifer L.

Babymouse : queen of the world! / Jennifer Holm and Matthew Holm

p. cm.

SUMMARY: An imaginative mouse dreams of being queen of the world, but will settle for an invitation to the most popular girl's slumber party.

ISBN 0-375-83229-7 (trade) — ISBN 0-375-93229-1 (lib. bdg.)

[1. Popularity—Fiction. 2. Imagination—Fiction. 3. Friendship—Fiction. 4. Mice—Fiction. 5. Animals—Fiction. 6. Cartoons and comics.]

I. Holm, Matthew. II. Title.

PN6727.H592B33 2005 741.5'973—dc22 2004051166

MANUFACTURED IN MALAYSIA First Edition 10 9 8 7 6 5 4 3 2 1

RANDOM HOUSE and colophon are registered trademarks of Random House, Inc.

FOR
MOM & DAD

RINGG!

RINNGGG!!!

FWAP!

ARE YOU GETTING UP, BABYMOUSE?

GLAMOUR
EXCITEMENT
ADVENTURE

IT WAS THE SAME THING EVERY DAY FOR BABYMOUSE.

WAKE UP.

GET DRESSED.
TUG
TUG
BRUSH HER WHISKERS.
TUG
TUG
STUPID WHISKERS.
EAT BREAKFAST.
VROOOOOM!
RUN TO CATCH THE SCHOOL BUS.
HEY!

WHERE WAS THE GLAMOUR?
THE EXCITEMENT?
THE ADVENTURE?

ALL BABYMOUSE HAD WAS AN OVERDUE LIBRARY BOOK AND A LOCKER THAT STUCK.

NNNGGHH!

IT WAS JUST ONE MORE THING SHE WAS STUCK WITH.

STUCK WITH SANITATION DUTIES.

BABYMOUSE, WOULD YOU MIND TAKING OUT THE TRASH?

STUCK WITH AN ANNOYING LITTLE BROTHER.

STUCK WITH HOMEWORK.

STUCK WITH CURLY WHISKERS.

BABYMOUSE DIDN'T HAVE A LOT OF EXPECTATIONS.

WELL, MAYBE JUST A FEW.

TIARA!

STRAIGHT WHISKERS!

ICE CREAM FOR LUNCH!

NO HOMEWORK!

QUEEN OF THE WORLD!

FAME!
FORTUNE!
TASTY SNACKS!
QUEEN BABYMOUSE! SMILE!
FOR ME?
MMM... CUPCAKES.

BLINK!

BUT EVERYONE KNEW WHO THE **REAL** QUEEN WAS...

...FELICIA FURRYPAWS.

, HI THERE, FELICIA, HOW ARE YOU TODAY? I HEARD WE
I FOR LUNCH TODAY. ISN'T THAT J
'S BETTER THAN THAT MEATL
E. YUCK! I WONDER IF IT EVEN HAS
ONALLY, I DON'T REALLY LIKE ANY F
RD "LOAF" IN IT. WELL, EXCEPT BR
COUNT? I GUESS NOT. OH—AND GU
HE NEATEST BOOK, ABOUT THIS
A WIZARD AND GETS TO GO TO
OOL. ISN'T THAT COOL? I WISH WE W
OL. THEN WE COULD LEARN TO DO MA
STUFF INSTEAD OF HAVING TO LE
CTIONS. FELICIA, WH OU LIKE

OKAY...
BE COOL...

TRAMPLE
FELICIA!
HOW DO YOU GET YOUR WHISKERS SO STRAIGHT?
I LOVE YOUR DRESS!
TRAMPLE
TRAMPLE
OOF!
TRAMPLE
HA!
HA!
HA!
BLAH!
HA!
HA!
THAT IS SO TRUE.
HA!
HA!
SIGH.
BABYMOUSE WOULD'VE SETTLED FOR BEING ASSISTANT QUEEN.

STILL, THERE WAS ALWAYS WILSON THE WEASEL.
HI, BABYMOUSE.
HI, WILSON.
LOCKER STUCK AGAIN?
YEP.
BAM!
THANKS.
NO PROBLEM.
THEY'D BEEN FRIENDS FOREVER.

KINDERGARTEN.
HIGHER!
UMPH!
FIRST GRADE.
MORE FROSTING!
SECOND GRADE.
HIGHER!
PUSH
THIRD GRADE.
JUST TWO MORE!
OOF!

FRIDAY NIGHT.
MY HOUSE.
ATTACK OF THE
GIANT SQUID.
COOL!

RINNGG!!
SEE
YOU
IN
CLASS.

I LOVE
MONSTER
MOVIES.

SPOOKY
FOG.
SSSSSSSS...

CLICK!

HEY! WHO
TURNED OUT
THE LIGHTS?

THIS IS KIND
OF SPOOKY.

WHAT WAS THAT?
TAP
TAP

AAAGGHH!!

BABYMOUSE

THE SQUID

IN MOUSE-VISION®!

FLING!
WAUGHH!!
EWWW...
SQUID SLIME

LATE AGAIN, I SEE. WHAT WAS IT THIS TIME? LOCKER TRY TO EAT YOU?
TYPICAL.

AH, SCHOOL.
BLAH BLAH BLAH.
COMIX
BRUSH BRUSH
THE JOY OF LEARNING.
ZZZZZZZZZZZZZZZZZ...
DETECTIVE STORIES
FILE FILE FILE
PSST.
?
DETECTIVE STORIES
PSST. PASS IT ON.
HMM...

BABYMOUSE
INVESTIGATIONS
It was a day like any other in the big city.
The name's Babymouse, Private Eye.
GATIONS
CREEAAAKK...
There I was, minding my own business.
The dame popped into my office like a bad case of the chicken pox.

Her straight whiskers should have tipped me off that she was trouble.

But in my line of work, you see it all.

She kept jabbering about some note.

LOOK, I NEED YOU TO PASS THIS NOTE ON.

I had my suspicions.

WHAT'S IT SAY?

But the dame clammed up.

JUST PASS THE NOTE, BABYMOUSE!
PASSING NOTES AGAIN, I SEE.
GULP!
WAY TO GO, BABYMOUSE.
PRINC
OFFI
MAYBE YOU SHOULD GIVE UP DETECTIVE WORK, BABYMOUSE.
SIGH.

LUNCHTIME. . .WHERE THE FOOD WAS DEFINITELY NOT FIT FOR A QUEEN— OR EVEN AN ASSISTANT QUEEN.

EWW.

MEATLOAF AGAIN? BLEAH!
PLOP!

NOT TO MENTION, SOMEONE WAS SITTING ON BABYMOUSE'S THRONE.

THERE'S NO ROOM, BABYMOUSE.

TYPICAL.

WHERE'S A PRINCE WHEN YOU NEED HIM, ANYWAY?

OVER HERE, BABYMOUSE! I SAVED YOU A SEAT.

HMM...
FAIRY TALES
TEETER
FWAP!
RATS.
ROLL
GET BACK HERE.
ROLL...

I'M HAVING A SLUMBER PARTY FRIDAY NIGHT.
?
A SLUMBER PARTY?
BABYMOUSE WONDERED IF SHE WOULD BE INVITED.
SCRUB SCRUB
IT WAS THE SAME OLD STORY...

I'M INVITED TO THE BALL!
Royal Invitation

WHAT ABOUT ME?
WITH THOSE WHISKERS? HA!

POOR BABYMOUSERELLA.
HA HA HA!
SIGH.

BABYMOUSE SURE COULD USE A LITTLE HELP HERE.
YEAH, I SURE COULD USE A LITTLE HELP HERE!

POOF!

COUGH COUGH!

HELP IS ON THE WAY!
DID SOMEONE ASK FOR HELP?
YOU'RE MY FAIRY GODMOTHER?

I PREFER "FAIRY GODWEASEL."

NOW HOLD STILL...
PWANG!

FOR A FAIRY GODWEASEL, WILSON WASN'T HALF BAD.

TRANSPORTATION HAD BEEN ARRANGED.

A BANANA?

THEY WERE OUT OF PUMPKINS.

THERE WAS ONE SMALL PROBLEM, THOUGH.

CLICK

HEY! GET OUT OF MY CARRIAGE!

YOUR CARRIAGE? THIS IS MY CARRIAGE. YOU'RE PULLING IT!

WHAT?!

IN "CINDERELLA," THE MOUSE PULLS THE CARRIAGE. DUH!
TYPICAL.
TRUDGE
TRUDGE
WELL, THAT IS THE WAY THE STORY'S WRITTEN.
WILL YOU BE QUIET?!

IT SEEMED LIKE EVERYONE WAS INVITED TO THE SLUMBER PARTY.

ALMOST EVERYONE.
HELLO IN THERE!
hello in there...

ANYBODY HOME?
anybody home?...

HELLO!
hello...

HUMPH!
do your homework...

BABYMOUSE KNEW THE SLUMBER PARTY WAS HER BIG CHANCE TO SHOW FELICIA FURRYPAWS HOW COOL SHE WAS!

. . .WHICH IS WHY MICE EAT CHEESE!

HA HA HA HA HA HA HA HA HA HA HA HA HA HA HA

I NEVER KNEW HOW COOL SHE WAS!

SHE COULD SEE IT NOW.

PLEASE SAY YOU'LL BE MY BEST FRIEND.
I SUPPOSE.

HER WHOLE LIFE WOULD BE DIFFERENT.

HOW DO YOU GET YOUR WHISKERS SO CURLY?

THEY'RE NATURAL.

CAN I BORROW YOUR DRESS SOMETIME? THE HEART IS SO STYLISH!
I KNOW.

THE NEXT MORNING.
NOTHING!

THIS LOCKER IS LIKE A BLACK HOLE!

HEY!

HELP!

SLAM!

BURP!

DEEP SPACE.

THE LIFE
OF A SPACE
EXPLORER
WAS A LONELY
ONE.

THEY HAD BEEN AWAY FROM EARTH FOR YEARS. THEIR MISSION WAS GRAVE.
LIVES HUNG IN THE BALANCE.
CAPTAIN, WE'VE CLEARED THE BLACK HOLE.
SET COURSE FOR ALPHA CENTAURI.
AFFIRMATIVE.

THEY DARED NOT FAIL.

NO! THE INVITATION TO FELICIA FURRYPAWS' SLUMBER PARTY!
UHH . . . MAYBE NOT.
CAPTAIN! THE ALARM IS RINGING!
BZZT!
THE ALARM?
BZZT!
BZZT!
ALARM

RINNNNNNNGGG!!!!!
BABYMOUSE! DID YOU HEAR ME? THE BELL FOR CLASS IS RINGING!
UHH . . . THANKS.
SEE YOU LATER.
THIS IS GOING TO BE THE BEST PARTY EVER!
ANYBODY WHO'S ANYBODY WILL BE THERE.
YEAH!
I JUST **HAVE** TO GET AN INVITATION TO THAT SLUMBER PARTY!
SLAP!

BABYMOUSE MADE PLANS.

COOL YOU

IMPRESS FRIENDS

HOW TO BE POPULAR

STEP #1.

I DON'T EAT CUPCAKES.

BUT THEY'RE REALLY YUMMY!

STEP #2.

I DON'T LIKE TO READ.

BUT IT'S REALLY EXCITING!

NEW BOOK

BABYMOUSE DIDN'T GIVE UP EASILY.

THERE HAS TO BE **SOMETHING.**

OPERATION: SLEEPOVER

~~1. CUPCAKE~~

~~2. BOOK~~

~~JOKE~~

~~COMPLIMENT~~

AND THEN IT HAPPENED.
PLEASE PASS UP YOUR BOOK REPORTS.

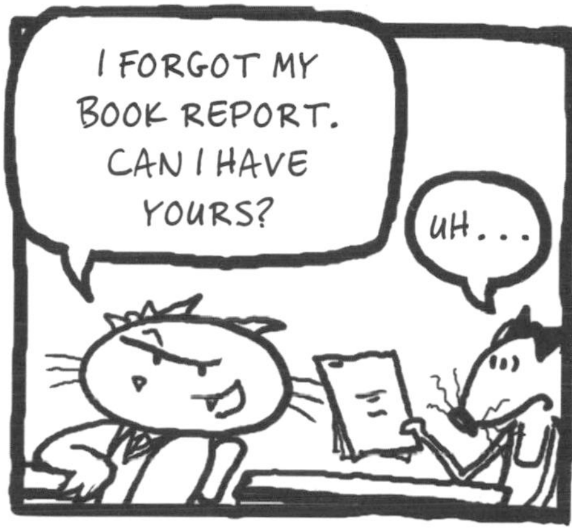
I FORGOT MY BOOK REPORT. CAN I HAVE YOURS?
UH . . .

YOU CAN COME TO THE SLUMBER PARTY . . .

BABYMOUSE KNEW WHAT SHE HAD TO DO.
OKAY!

AFTER CLASS . . .
SEE YOU FRIDAY.

I'M INVITED!

I'M INVITED! I'M INVITED! I'M INVITED! I'M INVITED! I'M INVITED! I—

UH-OH. LOOKS LIKE BABYMOUSE IS IN TROUBLE.

BABYMOUSE, CAN I SPEAK TO YOU ABOUT YOUR BOOK REPORT?
GULP!

I THOUGHT YOU DID YOUR BOOK REPORT . . .

I, UH, GUESS I FORGOT.
NOTE FROM TEACHER

MOM, CAN I GO TO FELICIA FURRYPAWS' SLUMBER PARTY FRIDAY NIGHT?
WELL...
BOUNCE
BOUNCE

WHOOSH!
THANKS!

BABYMOUSE DECIDED TO PACK RIGHT AWAY!

BABYMOUSE KNEW THE SLUMBER PARTY WOULD BE A GLAMOROUS EVENT.

NOW, WHAT SHOULD I BRING?

SHE HAD TO FIND THE PERFECT OUTFIT.

HMM...

TOO TIGHT.

GULP! . . .
CAN'T . . .
BREATHE . . .

TOO FLUFFY.
BLEAH!

TOO DANGEROUS!

WHA-

UH-OH

WHOA!

AAAAAAAH!
WHUMP!

TOO CONFUSING!
I'M DIZZY!

PERFECT!

FINALLY, THE DAY OF THE BIG SLUMBER PARTY ARRIVED.
SLAM!
SEE YOU TONIGHT. MY MOM'S MAKING CUPCAKES.
TONIGHT?
GO, SQUID!!

TUMBLE
WILSON! WAIT!

OW!
BONK!

WHAT ARE YOU GOING TO DO NOW, BABYMOUSE?
WILSON WILL UNDERSTAND, RIGHT?
RUB
RUB

THAT NIGHT.
READY TO GO, BABYMOUSE?
I THINK SO, DAD.

BABYMOUSE WAS EXCITED THE WHOLE WAY OVER TO FELICIA'S.

SHE HAD LOTS OF IDEAS ABOUT WHAT THEY WERE GOING TO DO.

SKYDIVING!

DINNER THEATER!

GO-KART RACING!

SNORKELING!

I CAN'T WAIT!

I'M HERE! LET THE FUN BEGIN!

BUT WHEN SHE GOT THERE, ALL ANYONE WANTED TO DO WAS TALK.

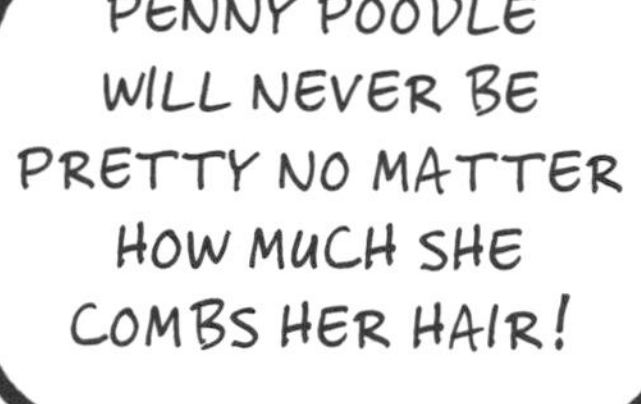

PENNY POODLE WILL NEVER BE PRETTY NO MATTER HOW MUCH SHE COMBS HER HAIR!

HA HA HA HA HA HA HA HA HA

AND TALK.
BLAH BLAH!
HA HA!
AND TALK.
BLAH!
YAWN!
HA HA HA!
THIS IS SO BORING. I WONDER IF WE'RE GOING TO PLAY ANY GAMES.
HMM...

SHE RODE ALONE.
OOH!
GASP!
HER FAITHFUL STEED WAS HER ONLY COMPANION.
SALOON
GOOD BOY.

FEW HAD MET HER.
WHAT'LL IT BE, FOLKS?
BUT HER NAME WAS LEGEND.
WHERE CAN I FIND A GAME IN THIS TOWN?

WILD "BABY" MOUSE!

THEY SAY SHE'S NEVER LOST A GAME!
OOH!
SHE'S SOOOO DARK AND MYSTERIOUS-LOOKING!
THE NAME'S BABYMOUSE.
WHAT'S YOUR GAME, BABYMOUSE?
YOU EVER HEAR OF A LITTLE GAME CALLED . . .
HEARTS?!

BUT FELICIA FURRYPAWS HAD OTHER THINGS IN MIND THAN GAMES.
LET'S GO TO MY ROOM.
LIKE BEAUTY LESSONS!
I JUST LOVE HOW YOU'RE DOING YOUR WHISKERS!
BRUSH
CURL

HOW HARD COULD IT BE?
LOOKS EASY ENOUGH.
OW!
SSSS!
CLUNK!
SSSSSSS...
MY RUG!
SORRY!

PAINTING HER NAILS HAD TO BE LESS DANGEROUS.
I JUST LOVE THIS COLOR!
OOH! ME TOO!
HMM...
I'M GOOD AT PAINTING!
HMM. STUCK.
STUPID BOTTLE!
NNGH!
POP!
RRRRAAAAAAARRRRHHH!!!!!

MEOW!
GLOOP!
BABYMOUSE!
MY FUR!
EEP! SORRY . . .

THE SLUMBER PARTY WASN'T TURNING OUT THE WAY BABYMOUSE HAD IMAGINED.

SIGH.
SMOOCH!
HE'S SO DREAMY!
THIS IS SO ROMANTIC.
THIS IS SO BORING.
WE'RE OUT OF POPCORN.
GO MAKE YOURSELF USEFUL, BABYMOUSE.
. . . AND BRING EXTRA BUTTER!

WHIRRRR
POP!
WHIRRRRRRR...
POP!
POP!
POP
POP
POP
POP
POP
POP
POP
POP
POP
WHOA!
POP POP
POP POP
POP
POP POP
POP POP
POP
POP
POP
POP
AAAAAAAA!!
POP
POP
WHIRRRRR
FOOF!
POP!
BOINK!
OW!
RUB
RUB
TYPICAL.

DRIP
DRIZZLE
DRIZZLE

I will love you forever, Lara. *SMOOCH*
AWWWWW!!!!
THAT WAS THE BEST MOVIE EVER!
I WONDER IF WILSON IS WATCHING MONSTER MOVIES.

DID YOU SEE GEORGIE THE GIRAFFE THROW UP AFTER LUNCH? HE IS SO GROSS! AND HIS NECK IS CROOKED!
HA HA HA HA HA HA HA HA!
CRACK!!

IT WAS A DARK AND STORMY NIGHT.

CRACK!

LADY BABYMOUSE HAD COME TO CASTLE WEASELSTEIN.

IT WAS SAID THAT DR. WEASELSTEIN CONDUCTED STRANGE EXPERIMENTS IN HIS TOWER LABORATORY.

I WONDER WHERE THIS LEADS?

SOME SPOKE OF A MONSTER.

DO NOT ENTER
STAY OUT!
DANGER: EVIL EXPERIMENTS UNDER WAY
LOOKS SAFE ENOUGH.

BUT LADY BABYMOUSE WAS NOT FAINT OF HEART.

AT LAST!
COME, SQUEAKGOR!
YES, MASTER.

HA HA HA
HA
HA
HA HA

BZZZT!
CLICK!

CRACK!

CRACK!

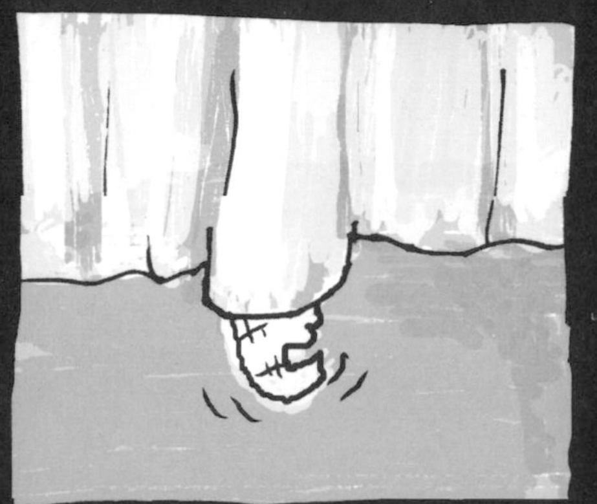

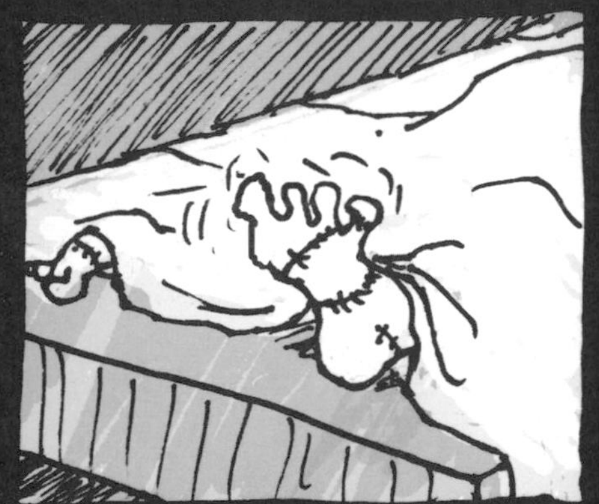

SHE'S ALIVE!

ALIVE!

GASP!

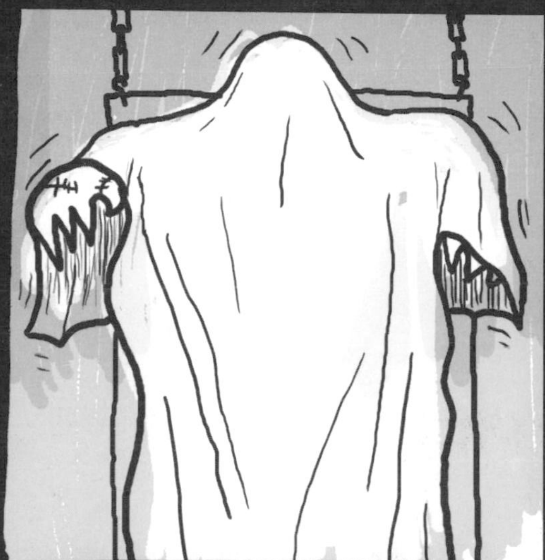

NNNGGGGHHH!!!

SWOOSH!

FELICIA-STEIN!

AAAAGGHH!!!

AND WILSON THE WEASEL IS SUCH A DOOFUS.

POP

HA HA HA HA HA HA HA HA!

OH NO!
WHAT HAD SHE DONE?

I GUESS BABYMOUSE FOUND ANOTHER BEST FRIEND.

BABYMOUSE COULDN'T IMAGINE NOT HAVING WILSON AS HER BEST FRIEND.
HA HA HA HA HA HA HA!
WILSON'S NEW BEST FRIEND
IT WOULD BE LIKE A CUPCAKE WITHOUT ICING.
BLEAH!
A BOOK WITHOUT A GOOD ENDING.
THAT'S IT?
THE END
A DRESS WITHOUT A HEART.
IT HAS NO STYLE!

HER LIFE WOULD BE SO COLD...
BRRR!
... AND LONELY.
STUPID PENGUINS.

WAIT A MINUTE...
WHAT IS IT, BABYMOUSE?
TASTY CUPCAKES!
SASSY STYLE!
EXCITING BOOKS!
WOW!
ADVENTURE!!
YIPPEE
GOOD FRIENDS!
MY LIFE IS GREAT!
I KNEW YOU'D FIGURE IT OUT EVENTUALLY, BABYMOUSE.
YOU DON'T HAVE TO RUB IT IN.
SORRY.

BABYMOUSE ALREADY **WAS** A QUEEN!
2
3

AND QUEENS DIDN'T TAKE ORDERS.
FELICIA FURRYPAWS, YOU STAND ACCUSED OF HIGH TREASON...
...OF TAKING HER MAJESTY'S BOOK REPORT, AND BEING MEAN IN GENERAL.
THEY **GAVE** THEM.
OFF WITH HER HEAD!
GASP!

BABYMOUSE! WHERE'S THAT POPCORN?
AND DON'T FORGET THE BUTTER!
HMM...
WHAT TOOK YOU SO LONG? DID YOU REMEMBER THE EXTRA BUTTER?

YEP!
GLOOP!
MEOW!

DUMP!
HEY!

WHAT ARE YOU DOING?
HEE HEE HEE HEE!
I HAVE SOMEWHERE MORE IMPORTANT TO BE.

YOU ARE SO WEIRD! I KNEW I NEVER SHOULD HAVE INVITED YOU!

DRIZZLE
SQUISH
SQUISH
SORRY I'M LATE.
THAT'S OKAY. THE MOVIE JUST STARTED.

IT WAS FUN...

BEING QUEEN OF THE WORLD!

POP!

B

I have agood friend alex

my friend tells me seckes

Laurynn Williams

HEY! BE SURE TO CHECK OUT MY NEW BOOK.

IT'S REALLY GOOD!
BABYMOUSE
OUR HERO
JENNIFER L. HOLM & MATTHEW HOLM

LET'S HEAR WHAT THE CRITICS HAVE TO SAY.
IT'S THE BEST ONE YET!
IT'S TOTALLY LAME.

I'M SURE IF BABYMOUSE WOULD ONLY APPLY HERSELF...

BABYMOUSE! BABYMOUSE!

BURP!
NOBODY LIKES A CRITIC, HUH, BABYMOUSE?

TYPICAL.

PSST!